A First Flight® Level Two Reader

For Ely, Bay and the Baby

FIRST FLIGHT® is a registered trademark of Fitzhenry & Whiteside

Rain, Rain

First publication in the United States in 1999.

Fitzhenry & Whiteside acknowledges with thanks the support of the Government of Canada through its Book Publishing Industry Development Program in the publication of this title.

Design by Wycliffe Smith.

Printed in Hong Kong.

10 9 8 7 6 5 4 3 2 1

Canadian Cataloguing in Publication Data

Kovalski, Maryann
Rain, rain

(A first flight level 2 reader)
ISBN 1-55041-518-2 (bound)
ISBN 1-55041-520-4 (pbk.)

I. Title. II. Series.

PS8571.O96R34 1999 jC813'.54 C99-930807-6
PZ7.K68Ra 1999

FIRST FLIGHT®

FIRST FLIGHT® is an exciting new series of beginning readers. The series presents titles which include songs, poems, adventures, mysteries, and humour by established authors and illustrators. FIRST FLIGHT® makes the introduction to reading fun and satisfying for the young reader.

FIRST FLIGHT® is available in 4 levels to correspond to reading development.

Level 1 – Pre-school - Grade 1
Large type, repetition of simple concepts that are perfect for reading aloud, easy vocabulary and endearing characters in short simple stories for the earliest reader.

Level 2 – Grade 1 - Grade 3
Longer sentences, higher level of vocabulary, repetition, and high-interest stories for the progressing reader.

Level 3 – Grade 2 - Grade 4
Simple stories with more involved plots and a simple chapter format for the newly independent reader.

Level 4 – Grade 3 - up (First Flight Chapter Books)
More challenging level, minimal illustrations for the independent reader.

“Two bathing suits,” said Jenny.
“Check!” said Joanna.

Jenny checked off *bathing suits.*

Joanna put the bathing suits
in the beach bag.

“Sun glasses, toys!” said Jenny.
“Check, check!” said Joanna.

“Beach towels,” said Jenny.
“Check!” said Joanna.
Jenny checked off *towels.*

Joanna rolled up the new
beach towels and put them
in the beach bag.

They would have fun
with Grandma tomorrow.

"Sun hats, water wings, games, and books," said Jenny.

"Check, check, check, and check!" said Joanna.

"One more thing," said Joanna.

"What is that?" asked Jenny.

"Sunshine in the morning!" said Joanna.

"I will write that down," said Jenny.

They were so excited, they wore their bathing suits to bed.

In the morning, Jenny could
not check off *sunshine*.

The sky was dark with clouds.
Rain hit hard against the
window.

"Oh no," said Jenny.
"No splashing Grandma today."

"And no picnic on our new beach
towels," said Joanna.

"Do you have all of your things
for the beach?" asked Grandma
when she arrived.

"But Grandma, look at the rain,"
said Jenny.

"Don't worry," said Grandma.
"You and Max will have
fun at the beach today."

"But Grandma, dogs are not
allowed at the beach,"
said Joanna.

"They are welcome at my beach,"
said Grandma.

7

On the street they waited for a taxi.
It rained, it plopped, it puddled.

"No splashing, no picnic, no fun,"
said Jenny.

“Wait and see,” said Grandma.
“Close your eyes and sing
with me.”

“Rain, rain, go away!
Come again another day!
Jenny and Joanna want to play!”

The taxi did not take them
to the beach.

The taxi took them to Grandma's.

In Grandma's kitchen, they made the best picnic ever.

Outside it dripped, it dropped, it drizzled.

They did not notice.

When the picnic was made,
they looked out the window.

Jenny and Joanna were sad.

"No splashing today," said Jenny.
"No picnic on the beach,"
said Joanna.

"Sing the 'Rain, Rain' song
while I tidy up," smiled Grandma.

"Rain, rain, go away!
Come again another day!
Jenny and Joanna want to play!"

But the rain did not stop.

They turned around.

Grandma was in her
bathing suit.

"This is not a bathing suit day,
Grandma," said Jenny.

"Follow me," said Grandma.

At the bathroom door, there was a sign:

They opened the door.

"Last one in is a rotten egg!"
said Grandma.

They splashed and played,
while the rain hit hard against
the window.

They did not hear it.

PLE
BE
NEAT

After their swim, Jenny and
Joanna played with Grandma's
dress-up box.

They had the best time
dressing up in Grandma's
old clothes.

When Grandma called them,
Jenny and Joanna went down
the hall.

They did not see Grandma, but arrows showed them the way.

At the living room door, they saw a sign:

Welcome to Grandma's beach.
Dogs allowed, it said.

They opened the door.
Grandma's living room was
brighter than a sunny day.

The picnic they had made
was set out on their new
beach towels.

"Welcome to my beach!"
said Grandma.
"Where the sun always shines!"

"This is the best beach!"
said Jenny.

"No sand in the sandwiches!"
said Joanna.

They had a nice picnic.

They played games.

Grandma read them a story.

"I have a song," said Joanna.

"Rain, rain don't go away!
Come down hard every day!
Jenny and Joanna want to play...
At Grandma's beach every day!"

Outside Grandma's window
the sun was shining.

They did not see it.